A LIKELY PLACE

A LIKELY PLACE

by PAULA FOX

illustrated by Edward Ardizzone

THE MACMILLAN COMPANY
NEW YORK

For Adam

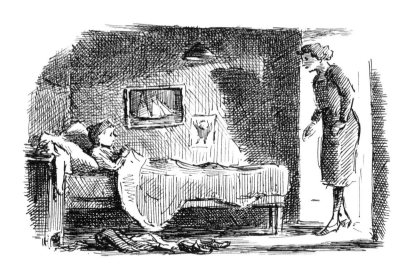

CHAPTER ONE

Everyone wanted to help Lewis. That's why he was thinking of running away.

But where could he go? He only had thirty-five cents left from his birthday present. His two Canadian dimes didn't count unless he could get as far as Canada.

Lewis was lying in bed watching the reflections of car lights move across his ceiling. He was thinking that if he could just remember the difference between *there* and *their* school wouldn't be so bad, when his mother came into his room.

"Are you still awake, Lewis?" she asked.

"Sort of," he said.

"Is there something on your mind, dear?"

What *was* on his mind? Lewis wondered. Skin, then brownish hair, then a woolen cap he had taken to wearing even when the weather was warm.

"Why, Lewis! You're still wearing that hat!" his mother exclaimed. "In bed, Lewis!"

"I forgot to take it off," he answered, which was only half true. He didn't especially want to explain that wearing the hat made him feel everything inside his head was in the right place.

"Well . . . " his mother said, hesitating at the door, "I think you should try to sleep."

He listened to his mother's footsteps going on down the hall, then he got up and walked over to his fish tank. The fish had been supplied by his parents to give him something to take care of so he could become responsible. They bored him to death.

When Lewis awoke the next morning, his youngest cousin was sitting on his bed. Lewis knew it must be Saturday. One Saturday every month his uncle and aunt and cousin came to visit.

"Where'd you get that hat?" asked his cousin.

"It's just a hat," said Lewis.

"A sleeping hat," said the cousin.

Lewis got up and began to get dressed. His clothes were in a heap where he had left them. His cousin watched as Lewis untangled a shoelace from a belt buckle and a shirt sleeve from a pants leg.

"You'll probably end up at Charlie Flocker's Farm," his cousin said.

"What's that?" asked Lewis.

"Oh, a place for people who hang their clothes on the floor and who sit down and don't do anything all day," replied the cousin.

"Who told you that?" asked Lewis.

"My mother told me," said his cousin. "And her mother told her, and her mother's mother——"

"Stop!" shouted Lewis. "Just tell me, what do they do there?"

The cousin crossed his eyes.

Lewis considered asking his own mother about Charlie Flocker. Probably she would say, "Oh, Lewis!" and give him an oatmeal cookie.

Lewis and his cousin went off to the kitchen to get some breakfast. His aunt and uncle and mother and father were drinking coffee at the kitchen table. They all looked up.

"I found the slipper you lost last month, Lewis," said his mother. "It was under the refrigerator."

"Lewis, do you have a plan for those batteries which are soaking in your spare fishbowl?" asked his father. "Because if you don't, I'll just remove them. A pity to stain the glass so."

That morning he and his cousin were taken to the museum. It was one of many places Lewis was taken to, even when he didn't care to go: the zoo, the playground, the beach, plays, concerts, ballets, museums.

Lewis' cousin found a big glass case full of swords. While they were deciding which ones they would like to have, Lewis' aunt called out, "Lewis, do look at this nice little sphinx! Imagine! It's three thousand years old!"

Then his mother called out, "Lewis, come and see this statue of a Roman senator. Doesn't it look like your uncle?"

He wondered why they left his cousin alone. Maybe it was because his cousin was still little. Lewis leaned up against a column until a museum guard scowled and motioned to him to move. His father hurried over.

"Are you all right?" asked his father.

"Fine," said Lewis. If he could have one wish it

4

would be to make people stop asking him how he felt —or telling him how he felt. "You must feel embarrassed because you spell so poorly," his teacher would say. "You must feel lonely on a rainy day like this with no one to play with," a friend of his mother would say. "It's too bad you live in the city where you only have a dirty, dinky playground to run around in," an absolute stranger would say. Lewis could have made a list a mile long of all the things people had told him he was feeling.

Just before his aunt and uncle left the museum to go home, his cousin whispered to him, "If you have a book and act like you're reading it, it's easier."

That night he took a book from the shelf, and while he was lying in bed looking at it, a hand turned it over to see the title. It was his mother's hand, but his father's voice said, "Hm . . . well . . . I see . . . uh-huh . . . well, well!"

Lewis spent most of Sunday thinking about running away. He wondered if anyone guessed. The doorman of the building across the street always seemed to be watching for him. He had heard of mind readers. Maybe the doorman was one.

His mother and father were walking back and forth in the living room exchanging sections of the Sunday paper. Lewis went out on the service stairs of the building to play solitaire. He liked it on the stairs. When the handymen who fixed things ran up and down from floor to floor, the noise was thunderous but Lewis didn't mind. The King of Hearts in his deck of cards had a large sooty heel print where one of the handymen had stepped on it. He could have erased the print with his gum eraser if he hadn't lost it.

The next morning as he passed the doorman on his

way to catch the school bus, the doorman called out, "Hello, kid. That's the ticket, kid! Get yourself educated!"

Why would the doorman say that to him, Lewis asked himself, unless he suspected that Lewis was up to something? Something like running away?

When he got to school, Lewis suddenly remembered the test the class was having the first thing that morning. But he had forgotten the name of the capital of Honduras. He stood in the corridor, knowing he had been marked absent. He was leaning against the wall, trying to think what to do, when the school principal walked up and put his arm around his shoulders.

"Lewis, you should be in class," he said.

"I know it," Lewis replied.

"We are trying to help children, Lewis," said the principal. "But they have to try too. Isn't that so?"

Lewis had heard some other questions like that one. "It's raining out, isn't it?" or "It's time for you to go to bed, isn't it?" or "Tomatoes are good for you, aren't they?" If he said *no* to any of these questions, grown-ups would look dizzy.

The principal led Lewis into the classroom. The principal smiled at the teacher, who smiled back. Lewis

didn't smile at anybody. He couldn't even remember where Honduras was.

When he got home that afternoon, his mother said she had something to tell him. In a few days, she said, it would be May, time for the annual trip to Chicago to visit relatives.

"We'll only be gone for a week," she said.

"Okay," said Lewis.

"You'll like Miss Fitchlow who is going to take care of you," she said.

"All right," said Lewis.

"Next year, we might even take you," his mother said. "If your schoolwork gets better."

He started for his room.

"Oh, Lewis, your three friends are waiting for you. Outside on the service stairs."

Lewis was glad to hear they were there and ran to the hall closet to get the old army blanket for them to sit on, because the stairs were cold. If they got cold they wouldn't stay to hear the ghost stories he read to them.

"Lewis! Wait!" his mother said. "How old are Henry and Betty Anne and Thomas?"

"Different ages," said Lewis.

"Oh, Lewis! I mean their average age."

"They're all around seven," Lewis answered.

"And you're going to be ten soon," his mother said. "Don't you think they're a little young for you? Wouldn't you rather play with children your own age?"

Lewis shrugged. He knew his mother was smiling only because she wanted him to do something different from what he was going to do.

"Are your friends all the same age?" he asked.

"That's not polite, Lewis," his mother replied.

"I was only asking," he said.

9

"The cat bites people," Miss Mowdith said as Lewis reached up a hand to pet it.

Then Lewis played his G. The cat jumped a foot in the air and ran for cover.

"Oh!" exclaimed Miss Mowdith. "What shall we ever do with you?"

That, Lewis gathered, was the problem. Even Henry had complained yesterday that Lewis' screeches weren't as scarey as they used to be.

On Thursday he handed in his weekly composition, and no sooner had his teacher looked at it than she dropped it on her desk.

"Lewis, you must learn to spell *their*. What will happen to you if you can't tell the difference between *there* and *their*?"

What *would* happen? Lewis wondered, as he wrote *their* fifty times. He was writing out the words so they formed a design like a snake on the lined paper. The teacher looked over his shoulder. "Lewis, you must learn the difference between a drawing class and a spelling exercise."

He put a note on the teacher's desk in which he wrote that her elbows looked like clam shells. He didn't sign it, but she seemed to know whom it was from.

"Not everyone in this world can have beautiful elbows," she said to him that afternoon.

That evening his father, who had heard about Lewis' spelling difficulties, said, "I should think a ten-year-old boy would be able to spell *their*."

"I'm nine," said Lewis.

"Going on ten," said his father. "Maybe I can help you."

But Lewis spelled *their* instantly and correctly.

"Any other words bothering you?" asked his father as he picked up Lewis' marbles from the living-room floor and handed them to him.

"Not yet," said Lewis.

"That's not what I heard," said his father.

"Heard," repeated Lewis, "h-e-a-r-d."

"All right, Lewis. That will do!" said his father.

Lewis would have liked Fridays to disappear from the week. But then, he supposed, he would have to have the weekly spelling test on Thursday. But to his surprise he spelled *their* correctly that morning. The teacher announced to the class that Lewis had, at last, learned the word. Lewis felt rather good about the whole thing except that he wished his classmates hadn't clapped so loudly.

Later his teacher took him aside, reminding him that

the spring reports would be due soon. She asked him what he was really interested in.

"Pygmies," said Lewis.

"Don't be funny," she said. Lewis looked down at his shoes. He had drawn a face on the toe of one with a marking pen. It was his right shoe. He had trouble remembering which was right and which was left. The face reminded him.

"Perhaps you're serious," the teacher said. "Would you like to make your report on pygmies? We're delighted you're interested in something."

Pygmies did interest him. He had seen a picture of a pygmy bridge in a magazine. It had been made from vines and then slung over a stream somewhere in Africa. There were several pygmies standing in the middle of the bridge with their arms around one another. They were all smiling.

"Could I do a report on something else?" Lewis asked. He wanted to keep the pygmies for himself. He didn't care to write all about the population of the pygmies or what they ate and what they learned in school or how they made a living. He didn't want to cut out and paste pictures of pygmies on white paper and put a cover around his report and read it to the class.

The teacher sighed. "Well. . . . Do a report on something," she said.

That very evening his father asked him what he liked best.

"A pygmy bridge," Lewis said, because it had been on his mind all day.

His father sighed too. "I don't understand you, Lewis," he said. His mother gave him a cookie and said they would bring him back a nice present from Chicago.

That's the way things were with Lewis.

CHAPTER TWO

As soon as it was May the weather seemed to change and grow warmer. Cats came out from behind garbage cans and wandered down the streets. The trees began to bloom. The doorman across the street unbuttoned his jacket, leaned against the wall and went to sleep standing up. Young flies flew through the classroom, and a bee crawled in one morning and swooped across the desks while all the girls screamed.

Lewis' mother and father would soon be leaving for Chicago.

"A little change of routine," his father said. "It'll be a change for you too, Lewis," he added.

Lewis wasn't interested in going to Chicago but he didn't want to stay home either. He hadn't met Miss Fitchlow yet. His mother said she was very nice. What could that mean? He hoped she wouldn't be like some of the other baby-sitters he had had. Mrs. Carmichael, for instance, had worn fat, purple slippers and had followed him around all day, and had even sat next to his bed at night until he had pretended to fall asleep. Mrs. Carmichael had hummed to herself all day long, always just one note. Perhaps that's where he had learned his special G.

Or Miss Fitchlow might be like Jake Elderberry, who sat on evenings when his parents went to the movies, and whose hair fell over his eyes and who thought he saw things behind the curtains. Or worst of all, she might be like Miss Bender, who weighed all the food she intended to eat on a little scale, and who washed everything a hundred times and who practically fell out the window scaring away the birds because, she said, they carried deadly germs in their feathers.

On Saturday morning while his parents were packing, Lewis went out for a walk. The sun was warm. He passed many baby carriages and children on tricycles. At the entrance to the park he saw dozens of dogs running around with their ears and tails up. They looked very busy. As he was watching them, he noticed a fat woman walking right toward him. She wobbled.

"Hello, honey," she said. "Knock 'em dead!" she added seriously, and her words ran together as though the sun was melting them.

He stared at her as she passed him and wobbled on down the street. Then, because he wanted to see what she would do next, he ran after her until people began to look at him and scowl.

"Running boys should do without their suppers!" croaked an old man, waving his cane at Lewis as he

ran by. Finally he couldn't see the lady anymore. He went back to the park entrance. He hadn't been in the park without his father or his mother. In another year, his father said, he would be allowed to go by himself if he had gotten to be a responsible boy by that time. It was, after all, a very big park. Lewis couldn't even see over the trees to the other side, where the river was. There was a zoo in it somewhere. There were lakes and paths and big rocks. Lewis thought that there must be a cave or two. He hoped he might be able to live in one for a while.

When he got back to the apartment, his parents were standing in the hall with their suitcases beside them. A tall, thin lady with a freckled face and reddish hair was there with them.

"This is Miss Fitchlow, Lewis," said his mother. "She has our number."

Miss Fitchlow laughed. She sounded like a horse. Lewis noticed his mother looked quickly at his father. Then his parents hugged him and reminded him of all the things he needed and all the things he should do as well as all the things he shouldn't do. Then they left.

"Say, pal, you've got a face on your left shoe," said Miss Fitchlow as they were standing in the hall.

"It's on my right shoe," Lewis said.

"Right you are!" Miss Fitchlow cried. "I ought to know that by now. Come with me! I'll show you something."

Lewis followed her into the living room, where Miss Fitchlow sank down instantly to the floor, her feet arranged in a peculiar way, crossed, each foot pointing straight up.

"Lotus position," she said. "Keep your back straight. Breathe deeply. Be quiet about it. Think nothing. Marvelous for the appetite. Do you like yoghurt? Some hate it. I brought my own brand. You can try it. Also pumpkin seeds. But honey is the greatest! What's the matter? Can't get your legs crossed? What do you expect? It takes time to learn, like everything else."

Lewis fell over backwards.

"What's this for besides appetite?" Lewis asked.

"Anything at all," Miss Fitchlow replied.

He ate a chop for dinner. Miss Fitchlow sloshed around a big bowl of yoghurt. It tasted queer to him— like undecided milk.

"How about some nuts?" she asked.

They ate nuts until there was a big pile of shells on the kitchen table.

"Something on your mind?" she asked. "So have I." But she didn't ask him what it was, or tell him what she was thinking about.

He decided to ask her a question he had been turning over for a week or so.

"Did you ever hear of Charlie Flocker?" he asked.

She rested her chin on her hand. "Charlie Flocker? Let's see. Say, I knew a Charlie Flocker in Bombay. He was there to study the rope trick. I don't think he ever could manage it. It's pretty tough to just disappear."

"Bombay?" asked Lewis.

"India," she said.

"He runs a farm," Lewis said.

"Not the Charlie I knew," said Miss Fitchlow. "He couldn't run a scooter."

"Maybe there're two of them," said Lewis.

"Possible, but not probable," said Miss Fitchlow.

"He runs this place for people who don't do anything," Lewis said.

"That's for me!" shouted Miss Fitchlow and laughed her horse laugh. Then she began to wash the dishes.

"I hate to dry," she said. "You dry, pal."

"I don't know how," Lewis said.

She handed him a wet plate and a towel. "Figure it out," she said.

He dropped one fork and when it clanged on the kitchen floor, Miss Fitchlow did a little dancing, snapping her fingers together and rolling her eyes.

The next morning Lewis found Miss Fitchlow in the living room lying between two chairs, her feet on one, her head on the other, the rest of her in-between.

"Pretty good, eh?" she said. "Took me years to learn this one. You can start your breakfast. I have another two minutes to go before I can get up."

Lewis went to the kitchen but there was nothing on the table. He drank a whole can of apricot juice and

toasted an English muffin, which he ate with peanut butter on it.

"How was it?" asked Miss Fitchlow from the door. She looked a little taller. He wondered if her morning exercise had stretched her.

"It was okay," said Lewis.

"What have you in mind for today?" she asked.

"I thought I'd go to the park," he said, hoping his parents hadn't told Miss Fitchlow he wasn't responsible yet.

"Pretty good," she said. "Cover the peanut butter. It'll get dry as a bone. No point in that."

He did.

"Not that fresh peanuts aren't better," she added.

The dogs in the park were not so busy today. Some of them were asleep, stretched out beneath the trees with their tails curled around them so they looked like neat packages. Lewis walked through the entrance. He would have been worried if he hadn't been so excited. He could just imagine his father smiling as he said, "Why, Lewis! Don't you remember that we asked you not to go into the park?"

Then he saw a small snake curling through the grass. He leaped for it. It wound itself around his wrist. A lady who was passing by uttered a little screech and hurried on. A man walked up to him.

"What have you there?" he asked.

"A snake," said Lewis.

"So I see," the man said, "but one must do better than that. It is known as DeKay's snake. Notice the chestnut color. Note the black dots along its sides."

The snake slid off Lewis' arm and disappeared beneath a bush.

"Easy come, easy go," said the man. Lewis walked on.

Everything in the world seemed to have a name.

He came to a fork in the path and, looking down at his shoes, turned right. Soon he came to a small square enclosed by trees, with benches all around a few yards of gravel. An old man was sitting alone on a bench. He wore a high, black hat and had on gloves. There was a large umbrella furled across his lap. Lewis observed him for a while. The old man was talking to himself. Although he spoke in a loud, clear voice, the words were in a language which Lewis didn't understand.

A boy zipped through the square on a bicycle. Lewis jumped back. The old man looked up.

"Too fast!" said the old man. "Square wheels would
have changed history." Lewis wasn't sure to whom he
was speaking.

"You got a bicycle too?" asked the old man. Lewis
looked around quickly. But there was no one in the
square except himself and the old man. He shook
his head.

"I only wish I had such a bicycle," the old man said,
sighing. "I'd ride it like a devil. Ride it, ride it all the
way home!"

Lewis looked at the umbrella so the old man couldn't tell that he was surprised.

"Who can tell?" said the old man. "It might rain."

Another mind reader, thought Lewis, and he started to leave the square.

"Wait!" cried the old man. "Don't you want to know where my home is? Have you no curiosity?"

Lewis halted. If he walked away, the old man might ask him where he was going. He might even tell him he shouldn't be in the park.

"Barcelona!" shouted the old man. "And I'll tell you something. If I could ride a bicycle in the first place, I could ride it across the Atlantic Ocean in the second place."

"Is that the capital of Honduras?" Lewis asked.

"Honduras!" exclaimed the old man. "Barcelona in Honduras," he repeated as if astonished. "Why—it's in Spain, dear friend. Come over here and sit down. I must tell you a thing or two."

Lewis sat down on the bench next to the old man.

"It is a large city, very splendid, on the Mediterranean Sea. Ships come to its harbor from all over the world, even from Honduras. In the middle of the streets there are *ramblas*. On those splendid *ramblas* a person can walk at any time of the day or night and nobody will knock him down with a car. In the afternoons after my work was done, I had a cup of chocolate so thick it had to be eaten with a spoon. Often I think to myself—what has happened, Emilio? Boys on bicycles make my brains rattle, and instead of chocolate in the afternoons, I sit here on this bench and try to compose myself and write a letter, and when it is too cold to sit here, I sit in my room and try to write this same letter."

"Who are you writing to?" asked Lewis.

The old man scowled. "To my son-in-law who married my daughter, Preciosa."

"Where does he live?" asked Lewis.

"In the same house I am," replied the old man.

"Can't you just tell him?" Lewis asked.

"Can you tell a rock? No! I will write. Then I must go home to Barcelona," said the old man.

"All right," said Lewis.

"It's all wrong," said the old man. "I been here three years. Observe my English! Beautiful! But I can't write it. What kind of mad language is it? You see a word and it's nothing like the way you say it. Sometimes I jump up and down on the newspapers and

Preciosa comes running and explains to me the stupid word I cannot understand because of this crazy spelling. The sound and the writing are not even cousins. In my language, it's intelligent. My name is Madruga. Spell it!"

"Me?" asked Lewis.

"You," said the old man.

Lewis spelled it.

"Perfect! You see?" asked the old man. "Even a person who does not speak can spell. What is your name?"

"Lewis."

The old man spelled: "L-U-I-S."

"No," said Lewis.

"Try another," said the old man.

"Cough," said Lewis.

"Ah!" exclaimed the old man. "Watch! C-O-F."

"Wrong," said Lewis.

"Naturally," said the old man. "Because it is un-reasonable, English. What can you expect?"

"Where did you have the chocolate?" asked Lewis.

"In the café," said the old man. "At a table beneath a small umbrella, out on the sidewalk where I could watch the people walking pleasantly on the *ramblas*. But now I have neither chocolate nor work. My son-in-law won't permit me. I am extraordinarily skilled. I make beautiful shoes, everything by hand. But he says I drop things. I have never dropped anything in my life. He says, 'Go read the newspapers.' What is in the newspapers? News. Nothing."

"What do you do?" asked Lewis.

"I come to the park and sit on this bench and think about this letter which I cannot write. I sit and sit. Then I go home and sit in my room. Then it is supper at a barbaric hour, 5:30. My son-in-law doesn't eat. How can he? He is watching me all the time. 'Pa,' he says, 'you are about to drop your spoon.'"

"What's his name?" asked Lewis.

"Charlie," replied the old man, looking sad.

"Charlie Flocker?" asked Lewis.

"What's that?" asked the old man.

"Nothing," said Lewis. Then he asked, "What's the letter for?"

"For telling Charlie what I think. Also my plans. He thinks I am too old to have plans," replied the old man.

They were silent for a little while.

"I suppose," the old man said at last, "that you can write this insane language, English?"

"Sometimes," said Lewis.

"Ah, I understand," said the old man. "It is like having fits, no?"

Lewis nodded.

"Would you do me the great favor of writing this letter?" asked the old man. He looked at Lewis with a serious expression. "I will tell it to you," he said, "and you will spell."

"Okay," said Lewis. "But I make mistakes."

"Think nothing of it," said the old man. "Could we begin now? I have paper and pencil in my pocket."

"I was going to look for a cave," said Lewis.

The old man looked disappointed.

"But I can do it tomorrow," said Lewis.

"I am very good at caves," said the old man eagerly. "And I can help you. That will be in exchange for the letter."

"All right," Lewis said.

The old man reached into his pocket and took out a pad of paper and a short yellow pencil.

"My esteemed son-in-law Charles," he began.

Lewis looked up at him. "How about 'Dear Charlie'?" he asked.

"Ah, that's better," said the old man. "Customs are different everywhere. Now, write: 'Sometimes I ask myself what am I? An old chair to gather dust in the corner? Me? A skilled shoemaker?' "

"Wait!" said Lewis. "You're going too fast."

The old man folded his hands over his umbrella and waited until Lewis was finished writing.

"Here's what I wrote," said Lewis shortly. " 'Dear Charlie, I don't want to sit in a corner. I want to make some shoes.' "

The old man smiled for the first time. A gold tooth shone in his mouth. "Very good," he said. "Now——"

But he was interrupted by the appearance in the

square of a large man in a green jacket. Lewis wondered whose hat he was wearing. It couldn't have been his own.

"Pa!" cried the man. "Pressy's got a big Sunday dinner all ready and here you are, stuck to that bench as usual. The spuds are burned and the peas are as hard as pebbles. Come on home now before something else happens!"

The old man whispered to Lewis behind his hand. "You heard? *Pressy!* My poor daughter!"

"Move, Pa!" said the man. "You ought to play with people your own age!"

The old man shouted rapidly in the same language Lewis had heard him speak when he first came to the square.

"Cut the cackle!" said Charlie. "Let's make time!"

The old man rose slowly to his feet and bowed to Lewis. "Perhaps we can continue tomorrow," he said gravely.

"It has to be later because of school," Lewis explained.

"At your convenience," said the old man.

"Pa!" bawled the large man.

"After three," Lewis said hurriedly.

32

"I will be here with the nothing newspaper," said the old man, and he twirled his umbrella and began to walk away.

"*Adiós,*" he called back over his shoulder.

When Lewis walked into his apartment, Miss Fitchlow was standing on her head in a corner of the hall.

"Good for the brains," she said.

CHAPTER THREE

LEWIS looked at the classroom clock only twice during the day. Each time, he was surprised to see how far the hour hand had advanced.

It was a strange Monday. He hardly knew he was in school because he was thinking so hard about old Mr. Madruga and about how he must finish all his work so he would not be kept in after school.

While he was looking up the word "shoemaker" in the classroom dictionary (in case he should have to use it in Mr. Madruga's letter), he found a number of other words he had not seen before. He learned, for example, that "shoo" was a sound used to frighten birds away, and that a "shogun" was a Japanese ruler.

"Why, Lewis!" cried his teacher. "You're using the dictionary!"

Lewis muttered "shoo!" under his breath.

"What?" asked the teacher.

"Spanish is easier to spell," he said.

"So it is," she agreed.

"What's your hurry, kid?" shouted the doorman as Lewis raced past him on his way home.

Miss Fitchlow was in the kitchen making carrot pudding.

"In case you want to see in the dark," said Miss Fitchlow, pointing to the pudding, "this guarantees it. Takes a bit of getting used to, though. How about a taste?"

"Wow!" said Lewis after he had taken a bite.

He waited for her to ask him what had happened in school. Perhaps she didn't really know where he had been most of the day.

"I was in school," he said.

"Ah!" said Miss Fitchlow. "The old daily double."

"I've got to go to the park now," he said.

"Okay," said Miss Fitchlow.

35

"What are you going to do?" Lewis asked.

"Meditate," she replied.

"What's that?" he asked.

"Clean out the attic," she said.

He thought about attics all the way to the square in the park. He thought of trunks and spider webs and old birdcages, the kind he had seen in his cousin's attic. Miss Fitchlow reminded him of agreeable things even though he didn't always understand what she was talking about.

Mr. Madruga was sitting on the same bench, his umbrella resting between his knees, a folded newspaper beside him. Lewis thought he was asleep. Then the old man looked up.

"Oho!" said Mr. Madruga. "My dear friend, I've made you something." He held out a bird made from newspaper. It was very small and had many paper feathers. It rested lightly on Lewis' palm.

"Thank you," he said.

"It's nothing," said the old man. "First, we will look for a cave."

Lewis was happy because Mr. Madruga had remembered.

They walked away from the square and down a

path. They passed a duck pond. The ducks were gath-ered around an old lady, through whose fingers grains of corn trickled.

"My ducks!" she cried as they walked by.

"Splendid!" said Mr. Madruga loudly. He whis-pered to Lewis, "Personally, I don't care for ducks."

The path they were following wound up a hill. At the top, where there were no trees, only a few gray rocks, they found a man staring up at the sun. They watched him a minute.

"What are you doing, please?" asked Mr. Madruga politely.

"I'm teaching myself to look at the sun," the man said.

"I can see the sun," Lewis said.

"No, you can't," said the man. "No one can see it. It's much too bright. But in a few days, I will be able to see it. Then I'll write a book. I'll call it, 'The Sun and I.' Or even better, 'I and the Sun.'" Suddenly he turned to look at them. "I can't see you yet," he said. "If you wait a minute until my eyes adjust, I'll describe my plan to you."

Mr. Madruga and Lewis tiptoed down the other side of the hill. When they looked back, the man had resumed his former position and was staring straight up at the sky.

"Can you see the sun?" asked Lewis.

"In a way," replied Mr. Madruga. "But I prefer to see the ground." Then he cried, "Look out for the infants!"

Just in time, Lewis saw two babies crawling at high speed directly toward him. Behind them, huffing and panting, came a lady in a white uniform.

"Gertrude! Matthew! This is positively the worst

you've ever been. Come back! Come back at once!" she cried.

But the babies kept right on going, so Lewis had to jump off the path to get out of their way.

"Devils!" muttered the lady as she passed them. Mr. Madruga was laughing so hard that he had to lean on his umbrella. Lewis began to laugh too.

"Maybe they'll escape," he said.

"No, no," said Mr. Madruga, wiping his eyes. "They won't escape. But they go very fast, no?"

"Will we find a cave soon?" asked Lewis.

"In time," said Mr. Madruga. "An empty cave is the most difficult thing of all to find." Then he turned off the path, holding back the branches of some thick bushes so that Lewis could follow him.

"Why are we going here?" asked Lewis.

"It's a likely place," answered Mr. Madruga.

How different the park looked here! No paths, no baskets for litter, no benches, no people. It was almost like the country. They walked through a small meadow of fresh spring grass. Ahead of them was another hill, but this one had no paths, and the rock faces were steep and smooth. Lewis ran ahead. Almost immediately he saw a cave opening. It was dark and jagged but wide enough even for Mr. Madruga. Lewis peered inside.

"Occupied!" shouted a voice.

"Inhabited!" shouted another.

"Positively filled to capacity!" cried a third.

Lewis sprang back.

"That was full," he reported to Mr. Madruga, who had waited for him in the meadow.

"There will be more," said Mr. Madruga.

The next cave was too small for Lewis to get his

head in and look around. The third cave was full of water. "For that one," said Mr. Madruga, "we would need a boat."

"We'll never find one," said Lewis, feeling discouraged.

"There!" said Mr. Madruga, pointing with his umbrella right in front of them. All Lewis could see was a tangle of vines.

"Lift them!" said the old man. Lewis pushed the vines away.

"What have you found?" asked Mr. Madruga.

"A big, empty cave," said Lewis.

It was large enough at the entrance for both of them to enter at the same time. There was a low ledge near the entrance upon which Mr. Madruga spread his newspaper. He sat down and waited while Lewis explored the cave.

Ten long strides took Lewis to the back wall. There he found a candle stub stuck into a soup can. He also found one black shoe with its laces. He must remember to look for someone wearing only one shoe on his way home. Underneath some dead leaves, he found a small, slightly damp booklet. The title was *Mosquito Control in Southeastern Delaware.*

Lewis returned to Mr. Madruga with the candle and the booklet.

Mr. Madruga took a kitchen match from his pocket and after lighting it with his thumbnail, lit the candle. Then he took out the notebook in which Lewis had started the letter to Charlie yesterday. Lewis put the paper bird down on the ledge between them.

They didn't really need the candle, because daylight was pouring in through the mouth of the cave. But it was nice to see the flame flicker in the light breeze.

"Shall we continue?" asked Mr. Madruga.

"Ready," said Lewis.

"You are content with your cave?" asked Mr. Madruga.

"Yes," said Lewis.

"In my country," said Mr. Madruga, "only the best dancers and the best singers live in caves."

"With furniture?" asked Lewis.

"With everything. Everything," answered the old man. Then he said, "Use the book you found for a little desk."

Lewis held up the pencil to show he was ready.

"Without work, I am nothing, nothing, an empty valise!" cried Mr. Madruga. "Charlie! You have

stopped me from looking for work. You tell me to 'take it easy,' and I ask myself, what does this mean——"

"Wait!" cried Lewis.

"I was carried away by my feelings," explained Mr. Madruga.

"Is this all right?" asked Lewis after thinking and writing a few minutes. Then he read, " 'You won't let me look for work.' "

"Yes, yes," said Mr. Madruga. "He even says I must not carry my umbrella. He says it's old-fashioned. Is rain old-fashioned? Also, it is pleasant to lean on. Imagine! He puts food into my mouth, turns out my light at night and holds my arm when we walk as if I were going to fall down on my knees!"

Mr. Madruga stood up and flourished his umbrella. The cave was not high enough for him to stand straight. Soon he calmed down again.

"Tell him," he said, "that I intend to go back to my own country as soon as I can find a ship. Tell him I would rather live in a cave with the gypsies dancing and singing and keeping me up all night than in his house. Also say thank you for his trouble and the many toothbrushes he has bought me while I have lived here."

After Lewis had finished the letter, he read it back to Mr. Madruga. It read:

Dear Charlie,

I don't want to sit in the corner. I want to make some shoes. You won't let me look for work. I am going home to Spain to live in a cave and stay up all night. Thank you for the toothbrushes.

"Excellent!" said Mr. Madruga. "You have the English style. The Spanish style is also very pretty.

Now put 'With many wishes for your continued good health, I am always your obedient servant,' and then I will sign my name."

"Could you just say 'good-bye'?" asked Lewis.

Mr. Madruga looked disappointed.

"I can't spell all those words," Lewis explained.

"In that case, yes. Put 'good-bye.' But in Spanish. *Adiós.* You can spell that?"

"Is this right?" asked Lewis, after thinking awhile.

"Of course," said Mr. Madruga. "But a little mark is required over the 'o' for emphasis."

Then Mr. Madruga signed his name, which took almost two entire lines.

"Is that just one name?" asked Lewis.

"Yes. It is nice to have such a name. When I am melancholy, I say my name over to myself and sometimes I feel cheerful again. *Emilio del Camino de Herrera de Santiago Martínez y Madruga.*"

The candle went out.

"Will you hand him the letter?" asked Lewis.

"No," replied Mr. Madruga. "I will leave the table after the soup. I will put the letter next to his plate. Then I will go to my room and wait until he has read it."

"Will you come to the park tomorrow?"

"If not tomorrow, then the next day. Then I will tell you the news. Who knows what will happen? I may be put out on the street like an old table. In that case, of course, I will defend myself with the umbrella!"

Lewis buried the remains of the candle in a pile of leaves at the back of the cave. He poked the mosquito book in a crack in the wall. He placed the paper bird on a little projecting shelf, where the wind could not blow it away.

"*Adiós,*" Lewis said to Mr. Madruga.

"*Adiós, amigo,*" replied Mr. Madruga.

46

After supper that evening, Miss Fitchlow told Lewis
a story about an owl who chased a mouse all over the
world, through jungles and cities, across deserts and
mountains, flying, riding on the masts of ships, even
hiding in freight cars.

"Why did the owl want that special mouse?" asked
Lewis.

"He had an *idée fixe*," said Miss Fitchlow.

"What's that?" Lewis asked.

"An idea that a person, or a bird, can't get rid of," explained Miss Fitchlow. She said that by the time the
owl had caught up with the mouse, the mouse had
become a plump, smart, giant mouse, very strong in the

legs because of all the running it had had to do to escape the owl.

"Then what happened?" asked Lewis.

"Nothing much," said Miss Fitchlow.

"Did he eat it?" Lewis asked.

"Did who eat what?" she asked.

"The owl eat the mouse?"

"The owl gave up mice and rats and became a vegetarian," said Miss Fitchlow.

"Why?"

"Discretion is the better part of valor," said Miss Fitchlow, "which means that if your dinner is bigger and tougher than you are, you'd better change your diet."

"Oh," said Lewis.

"I feel a cartwheel coming on," said Miss Fitchlow. "Make way!"

And with that, she did a double cartwheel across the living-room floor.

CHAPTER FOUR

Mr. Madruga was not in the park Tuesday or Wednesday or Thursday. At first, Lewis was very disappointed. Perhaps Mr. Madruga hadn't liked the letter Lewis had written for him. Perhaps he had just forgotten about him.

Of course, Charlie might have given him errands to do or might have made him read all the newspapers. Charlie might have decided he didn't want Mr. Madruga to go to the park anymore. Or else the old man might have found a ship to take him home. Perhaps he was, even now, drinking his chocolate in a café and watching people walk on the *ramblas*.

Still, Lewis had his cave.

Every afternoon, after he had checked the square to make sure Mr. Madruga was not there, Lewis went to the cave. Wednesday, he had seen another DeKay's snake near the entrance and had wondered if it was the same one he had seen his first day in the park.

Miss Fitchlow had been starchy about matches so he was unable to light the candle—not that he really needed it.

"Fire is sacred, my boy," Miss Fitchlow had said. "Like most sacred things, it tends to get easily out of hand."

Lewis had a good time in the cave, although he missed Mr. Madruga. He furnished it with a shoebox for interesting stones and bottle tops, a box of saltines in case he got hungry, along with several handfuls of nuts Miss Fitchlow had given him, and the blanket he had used for reading to the children on the service stairs. The bird was still on the ledge, although its paper feathers had wilted a little.

To pass the time, he read the booklet about mosquitoes in Delaware. He thought maybe he could use it for a report for the class.

He wondered if he could stand on his head without

Miss Fitchlow there to catch him if he fell over. He smoothed out a place on the dirt floor of the cave and covered it with leaves. The first time he tried he fell on his face. The second time he managed to get himself up, his legs straight and pointed up at the cave's roof. Then he let himself down in sections like a telescope and assumed the lotus position, breathing deeply. After that he felt quite light-headed.

On Thursday a small dog wandered into the cave. It was extremely friendly and it ate a number of peanuts from Lewis' hand. On the dog's collar tag Lewis read: "My name is Myra. I belong to Mr. Klopper."

"Myra," said Lewis. The dog wagged her tail.

"I bet somebody is following you," Lewis said. "I bet you're not even supposed to be in the park."

Myra wagged her tail.

"Say something," said Lewis.

Myra gave a low bark.

"I can spell anything," Lewis said. "Even that!"

Myra barked again.

"R-O-O-F," Lewis spelled. "Don't you know any other words? You're not responsible, Myra, old dog. You shouldn't be allowed out without a keeper. Take a letter, Myra. Ready? 'Dear Mr. Klopper, you shouldn't smile at Myra when you want her to stop doing something like chewing up the rug. Just tell her. Also, don't wake her up in the middle of the night to ask her what she's thinking about. It will make her have stiff brains.'"

Myra jumped up and licked Lewis' chin.

"Calm yourself," Lewis said sternly.

Myra drifted away after she and Lewis had finished the peanuts. It was pleasant to have guests dropping in.

After Myra left, Lewis began to feel sad again thinking about Mr. Madruga and wondering where he was. He tried saying the old man's name over to himself, but he could only remember half of it.

He went home earlier that afternoon. He walked up the service stairs thinking that maybe he'd find Henry or Thomas or Betty Anne to read to, but he only found Henry sitting outside his own door with an apple core in one hand.

"You don't read to us anymore," Henry said reproachfully.

"I have other things to do than read to you all the time," Lewis said. "Anyhow, you ought to learn to read yourself."

"I can read," Henry said in a sulky voice. "But I want to hear about the monkey's paw."

"You have heard about that a thousand times," Lewis said. "Read it yourself."

"I'll get somebody else to read it to me," Henry said.

"You're just a silly little kid," said Lewis crossly. Henry popped the apple core in his mouth and made a face at Lewis.

Lewis ran up to his own floor.

"I want to hear about that monkey," yelled Henry.

Lewis leaned over the railing and looked down at Henry.

"I'll haunt you myself," he said.

Henry giggled.

"Feeling spindly?" asked Miss Fitchlow that evening.

Whatever that was, Lewis guessed it was the way he was feeling.

"Cheer up!" said Miss Fitchlow. "The worst is yet to come!" With that, she gave a loud horse laugh. Then she showed Lewis how to do a cartwheel.

After a few moments of cartwheeling, Lewis did feel better. He told Miss Fitchlow all about Delaware's mosquito problems.

"Mercy!" she exclaimed. "I had no idea!"

He felt even better.

To Lewis' surprise, the word "mosquito" turned up in Friday morning's spelling test. He got it right. Better yet, the teacher didn't mention that he had gotten it right.

His plan was to go straight to the park after school. If Mr. Madruga wasn't there, he would go home. He didn't feel like visiting the cave today.

But when he got to the square, he saw Mr. Madruga sitting on his old bench. It was drizzling a little and Mr. Madruga had opened his umbrella.

"Well, well, dear friend. I'm so glad you came," said the old man. "I was afraid you might have forgotten me or thought I had gone away."

"I came every day," said Lewis.

"I thought you would, despite some doubts," said Mr. Madruga. "You are a good friend. Now. Let me tell you the news. My letter—no!—*our* letter astonished Charlie. Even Preciosa was astonished. I put the letter next to his plate, just as I said. Then from my room, I heard much crying and shouting and then a long silence. Then I hear the footsteps, then little taps at the door. I open the door. They are standing there. They don't wish me to go, they say. It would make them too sad if I went back to Barcelona. What could I do? Of course, I said I would stay."

The old man stood up and began to pace back and forth excitedly.

"But now, the big event!" he cried. "Charlie has a friend who has an uncle who is also a shoemaker. I have a job! The old man who worked for the uncle has now gone back to Italy so now the uncle needs a new old man. I am the new old man! Splendid, no?"

"Yes," said Lewis.

"Monday, everything begins," said Mr. Madruga. "I must go home now to shine my shoes and brush my hat and press my suit. I wish to give you a gift for your great help. Take this umbrella which my father gave me. Note the carved handle. It is a Spanish dragon. It is said such dragons used to live in Catalonia. Who knows? Perhaps they once did."

Mr. Madruga held out the umbrella. Lewis took it and then shook Mr. Madruga's hand.

"Thanks," he said.

"Until we meet again," said Mr. Madruga. *"Hasta la vista!"*

"Adiós," said Lewis.

When he got home, he saw that there were two suitcases in the hall. A minute later his mother, his father and Miss Fitchlow appeared. His mother kissed him and his father squeezed his shoulder.

"Are you all right?" asked his mother.

"All right!" exclaimed Miss Fitchlow. "Why, he is extraordinarily well coordinated, having managed some very difficult Yoga exercises right off. He is also the best-informed person on Delaware mosquitoes I have ever met."

"Well!" said his father.

"Why, Lewis!" said his mother.

Then his father noticed the umbrella which Lewis had furled and was leaning on.

"Where did you get that?" asked his father.

"A friend of mine gave it to me," said Lewis.

"But it's almost twice as big as you are," said his mother.

"I'll get bigger," said Lewis.

"Right!" said Miss Fitchlow.